Charles King

Trumpeter Fred

A Story of the Plains

Charles King

Trumpeter Fred
A Story of the Plains

ISBN/EAN: 9783743400153

Manufactured in Europe, USA, Canada, Australia, Japa

Cover: Foto ©Andreas Hilbeck / pixelio.de

Manufactured and distributed by brebook publishing software (www.brebook.com)

Charles King

Trumpeter Fred

TRUMPETER FRED

A STORY OF THE PLAINS

BY

CAPTAIN CHARLES KING, U. S. A.

AUTHOR OF " FORT FRAYNE," " AN ARMY
WIFE," ETC.

ILLUSTRATED

F. TENNYSON NEELY

PUBLISHER

NEW YORK   CHICAGO

1896

CONTENTS.

TRUMPETER FRED.

TRUMPETER FRED.

CHAPTER I.

A DANGEROUS MISSION.

THERE were only thirty in all that night when the troop reached the Niobrara and unsaddled along the grassy banks. Rather slim numbers for the duty to be performed, and with the captain away, too. Not that the men had lack of confidence in Lieutenant Blunt, but it was practically his first summer at Indian campaigning, and, however well a young soldier may have studied strategy and grand tactics at West Point, it is something very different that is needed in fighting these wild warriors of our prairies and mountains. Blunt was brave and spirited, they all knew that; but in point of experience even Trumpeter Fred was his superior. All along the dusty trail, for an hour before they reached the ford, the tracks of the Indian ponies had been thickly scattered. A war party of at least fifty had evidently gone trotting down stream not six hours before the soldiers rode in to water their tired and thirsty steeds. No comrades were known to be nearer at hand than the garrison at Fort Laramie, fifty long miles away, or those guarding the post of

Fort Robinson, right in the heart of the Indian country, and in the very midst of the treacherous tribes along White River. And yet, under its second lieutenant and with only twenty-nine "rank and file," here was "B" Troop ordered to bivouac at the Niobrara crossing, and despite the fact that all the country was alive with war parties of the Sioux, to wait there for further orders.

"Only twenty-nine men all told and a small boy," said Sergeant Dawson, who was forever trying to plague that little trumpeter. It was by no means fair to Fred Waller, either, for while he was somewhat undersized for his fifteen years, his carbine and his Colt's revolver were just as big and just as effective as those of any man in the troop, and he knew how to use them, no matter how hard the "Springfield" kicked. He rode one of the tallest horses, too, and sat him well and firmly, notwithstanding all his furious plunging and "buckings," the day that Dawson slipped the thorny sprig of a wild rosebush under the saddle blanket.

From the first sergeant down to the newest recruit, all the men had grown fond of little Fred in that year of rough scouting and campaigning around old Red Cloud's reservation—all of them, that is to say, with the possible exception of Dawson, who annoyed him in many ways when the officers or first sergeant did not

happen to be near, and who sometimes spoke sneeringly of him to
such of the troopers as would listen,
but these were very few in number.

Fred was the only son of brave
old Sergeant Waller, who had
served with the regiment all over
the plains before the great war
of the rebellion, and who had
been its standard-bearer in many
a sharp fight and stirring charge
in Virginia. Now he carried two
bullet wounds, and on his bronzed
cheek a long white seam, a saber
scar, as mementoes of Beverly
Ford, Winchester, and Five Forks,
and through the efforts of his war
commanders a comfortable berth
as ordnance sergeant had been
secured for him at one of the big
frontier posts along the railway.

Fred was the pride of the old soldier's heart, and nothing would do but that he, too, must be a trooper. The boy was born far out across the plains in sight of the Chihuahua Mountains, had fellowed the regiment in his mother's arms up the valley of the Rio Grande to the Albuquerque, then eastward along the Indian-haunted Smoky Hill route to Leavenworth. When the great war burst upon the nation little Fred was just beginning to toddle about the whitewashed walls of the laundresses' quarters—his father was Corporal Waller then—and his baby eyes were big as saucers when he was carried aboard of a big steamship and paddled down the muddy Missouri and around

by Cairo and up the winding Ohio
to Cincinnati. He was even more
astonished at the railway cars
that bore the soldiers and a few
women and children eastward and
finally landed them at Carlisle.
There at the old cavalry barracks
the little fellow grew to lusty boy-
hood, while his father was bear-
ing the blue and gold standard
through battle after battle on the
Virginia soil. And when the war
was over and the regiment was
hurried out to "the plains," and
again to protect the settlers, the
emigrants, and the railway
builders from the ceaseless
assaults of the painted Indians,
little Fred went along, and his
soldier education was fairly begun.

Old Waller was now first ser-

geant of "B" troop. The regimental commander and most of
the officers were greatly interested in the laughing, sun-tanned,
blue-eyed boy, who rode day after
day on his wiry Indian pony along
the flanks of the column, scorning,
though barely seven years old, to
stay in the wagons with the
women and children. Everybody had a jolly word of greeting
for Fred, and kind-hearted Captain Blaine set his "company
tailor" to work, and presently
there was made for the boy a
natty little cavalry jacket and a
tiny pair of yellow chevrons.
"Corporal Fred" they called him
then, and, though he strove hard
not to show it, grim old Sergeant
Waller was evidently as proud

and pleased as the child. He taught the little man to "stand attention" and bring up his chubby brown hand in salute whenever an officer passed by, and most scrupulously was that salute returned. He early placed the boy under the instruction of the veteran chief trumpeter, and made him practice with the musicians as soon as he was "big enough to blow," as he expressed it. And then, too (for there were no army schools, or schoolmasters in those days), regularly as the day came round and the sergeant's morning duties were done, he had his boy at his knee, book or slate in hand, patiently teaching him the little that he knew himself, and wistfully looking for some better instructor.

CHAPTER II.

THE OATH OF ENLISTMENT.

T was while stationed at old Fort Sanders that Waller's enthusiastic devotion to his new captain and his captain's family began. The former troop commander was ordered to the retired list, broken down by wounds, and the senior lieutenant stepped into his place. Waller bade farewell to his old captain with tear-dimmed eyes—they had served together for over fifteen years—and with much inward misgiving, but

not the faintest outward show
thereof, saluted the new arrival,
a young officer but a soldier
through and through ; it was not a
week before the sergeant had fully
satisfied himself as to that. Presently the new captain's family
reached the fort and took up their
abode ; a fair-haired, blue-eyed
young mother with two children,
a boy and a girl, the eldest being
three years younger than Fred ;
and then began another and
strong interest.

That very winter scarlet fever
devastated the fort. Few children escaped the scourge. There
were a dozen little graves in the
cemetery out on the prairie when
the long winter came to an end.
There were two or three larger

graves, and one of these held all that was mortal of Fred's loving mother; he and his stern, sad-faced father were now alone in the world.

And Captain Charlton's little household had not been spared. It was among the officers' quarters that the pestilence had first appeared. Frank and Florence Charlton were among the children earliest stricken. The servants fled the house, as frontier servants will, and their place was promptly supplied by Mrs. Waller. She and her husband would listen to no remonstrance, and Mrs. Charl-ton, overwhelmed with care and dread, was only too glad to have the strong, cheery army woman's help. Over the little brown cot-

tage the shadow of death hovered
for days before it was lifted and
borne away, and when at last all
danger was over and all was again
all hope and peace the sergeant's
wife went back to her own humble
roof across the parade, and there
suddenly sickened and died.
When the scourge was finally
swept from the garrison and the
soft winds began to blow from the
South, the stricken old soldier was
glad of the chance to go with his
troop into the field-service, and
was almost happy in one thing.
Mrs. Charlton had taken his boy
as one of her own, and each day
she was teaching him faithfully
and well. When the troop rode
away from Sanders Fred was left
behind to occupy a little room

under the captain's roof. "Remember, sir, you are sergeant of the guard, and that house and that household are your special charge for all summer long," were Waller's parting words to his boy.

Regularly as the mail reached the troop during its summer scouting Captain Charlton's home missives had their messages for Sergeant Waller ; and soon, to his unspeakable joy, letters all his own, addressed in a round boyish hand that grew firmer every week, began to come as his share of the welcome package. Never would he presume to ask for news, yet the captain was not slow to notice how old Waller was sure to be busy close at hand when the home letters came, and prompt to

ADDRESSED IN A ROUND BOYISH
HAND.

answer, and with soldierly salute
to stand erect before his young
commander and strive not to show
the pride and delight that tingled
in every vein at the glowing words
in which Mrs. Charlton told of his
boy's rapid progress and his devotion to her and the children. His
lip would quiver uncontrollably
and his eyes fill; his hand might
tremble as it touched the brim of
his scouting hat, but the salute
was precise as ever.

"I thank the captain, and beg
to thank the captain's kind lady,"
was his invariable formula on such
occasions. "I hope the boy will
always do his duty."

And then he would face about
and stride away with his head very
high in the air and his eyes blink-

ing hard, and almost immediately his voice would be heard sternly berating some trooper whose horse had tangled himself in his lariat, or whose " kit " was not stowed in proper shape about the saddle. It was his way of striving to hide the joy those messages brought him, and the men were quick to see through it all, and little " Reddy " Mulligan, reprimanded for the third time within a fortnight, started a laugh all through the bivouac by his whimsical protest :

" It's more good news you've been getting from Fred, sergeant, dear ; isn't it now ? Faith, I wish he'd play ye a thrick wanst in a while, like other byes. Maybe thin I'd be mintioned to the captain for a corporalship." And for once the veteran turned his back on the laughing troop conscious of defeat.

In '74 old Waller changed the yellow stripes and diamond of the first sergeantcy for the crimson and the star of the ordnance, and the troopers, one and all, said good-by to him with infinite regret. Perhaps Dawson, who was next in rank, may be excepted. He confidently expected to be promoted in Waller's place. But though a dashing soldier and a smart non-commissioned officer, he was not the stanch, reliable man the captain needed, and proved it by celebrating Waller's promotion in a very boisterous and unseemly manner. It was plain that he had been drinking heavily, and though Captain Charlton saved him from arrest and court-martial he would not promote him, and plainly, though privately, told him why. The troop knew it was for this reason, but Dawson swore it was all on account of Waller's influence against him when Sergeant Graham was named in regimental orders as the old veteran's successor.

That same summer, with firm hand and glistening eyes, Waller signed his consent to the enlistment of his son as trumpeter in the old troop. How he watched the boy's glowing face as the oath of enlistment, so often lightly spoken, was solemnly repeated, and Fred was bound to the service of his country. How he trembled from head to foot when, but a few weeks afterward and in the dead of night, Charlton and his men hurried forth to intercept a band of Indians who had swooped down upon the herders south of Laramie Peak. Waller could hardly buckle the cantle-straps of Fred's saddle as the little fellow, all eagerness, was bustling about his horse in the dim light of the stable lanterns. Yet when the captain and Lieutenant Rayburn came trotting briskly down the roadway and the men were silently "leading into line," it was the old sergeant's hand that grasped the boy's left foot and swung him lightly into his seat.

"Whatever happens, sir, mind you keep close to the captain," was his parting injunction to his boy. Then his heels came together with the old cavalry "click" and his twitching fingers were stiffened as they went suddenly up in salute to Mr. Rayburn, who bent down from his saddle to say that they would try and take good care of Fred. . But Waller· answered :

"I thank the lieutenant. The boy is a soldier now, sir. He must take his chances with the rest." Then with one lingering clasp of the trumpeter's hand, "Join your captain," he ordered, and turned away into the darkness. • But the sentry on No. 6 bore witness to the fact that the ord-

nance sergeant never went to bed
again all that night, and the men
sent to unload and store the ammunition that came next day from
Rock Island Arsenal declared that
old Waller was gruffer than ever.
All the next night too, he was
awake, waiting, watching for tidings from the North. Nothing
came until sunset of the second
day, just as the whole command
was turning out for retreat parade,
and then Corporal Rock rode
in with dispatches and trotted
straight to where the commanding
officer was standing in front of
the adjutant's office. All eyes
were upon him as he threw himself from the saddle and handed
the packet to the colonel. Half
a dozen officers hastened to join

their commander as he tore it
open. The piazzas of the officers'
quarters were quickly alive with
ladies and children, breathlessly
eager to hear the news. The colonel's orderly was seen hastening
to the surgeon's house — that
looked ominous — then Rock
remounted ; trotted to Captain
Charlton's gate, where Mrs. Charlton was tremblingly awaiting him.
" It's all right, ma'am," he hastened
to say. " Leastwise the captain's
safe, but Mulligan is shot—and
Ryan and Sergeant Frazer." She
hurried in the house with the
precious letter he placed in her
hands, and while several ladies
hastened to join her, the messenger returned to the office.

All this while Sergeant Waller

had stood like a statue under the tall white flag-staff where the non-commissioned staff assembled at retreat, watching every move with dry, aching eyes, and a face gray as his mustache.

CHAPTER III.

A ROBBER IN CAMP.

THE trumpet played the retreat, the sunset gun thundered its good-night to the god of day; the adjutant hurried over and received the reports of the companies, the staff, and band, and then a messenger came running to them : "Mrs. Charlton wants you, Sergeant Waller. Fred's all safe, but they had a sharp fight."

The old man could not trust himself to speak. "Listen to this, sergeant," exclaimed Mrs. Charlton, as she hurried through the little group of ladies at her doorway, and looked up in his face with tear-dimmed eyes:

"Tell Waller that in a running fight of four miles Fred rode close at my heels and no man could have shown more spirit or less fear. I am sure it was a shot from his carbine that tumbled one war pony into the Laramie; and every call he had to sound rang out clear as a bell. I'm proud of the boy."

Waller's face was twitching and working; he cleared his throat and tried to speak; he dashed his hand across his eyes and ground his heels into the gravel of the walk; he heard the kind and gentle voices of the ladies joining in the chorus of congratulation, but he could not see their faces; a mist had risen before his eyes. Even the old formula, "I thank the captain's lady," had deserted him. He mumbled some inarticulate words, and then, in dread of disastrous breakdown, turned suddenly away and strode across the drive. More than one woman was in tears. There was not a ripple of faintest laughter when it was seen that in his blindness the old sergeant had collided with the tree box at the edge of the acequia. Straight to his humble quarters he went; but they were beautiful to him, radiant with the light of joy, pride, gratitude, and love that beamed and burnt in his honest heart.

And now, a year later, all the cavalry was in the field. Gold had tempted explorers and miners innumerable to the Black Hills of Dakota—Indian land by solemn treaty. The Government warned the invaders back, but to no purpose. The Indians swarmed from the agencies and massacred all whom they could overpower. Charlton's troop had early been hurried up to Red Cloud, and now with others was engaged in the perilous work of patrolling the trails around the Indian haunts.

Two months of hard and most exciting work had they had, and still the troubles were not over; and then just after the paymaster with his iron safe and bristling escort had paid the outlying posts a visit, and Captain Charlton had been ordered in with him to attend a court-martial at Fort Laramie, there came a week that no man in " B " troop ever forgot.

Mr. Rayburn had been wounded and was in the hospital at Fort Robinson. Twenty of the men were away on escort duty, and so it happened that only young Lieutenant Blunt and about thirty troopers were left at the camp just west of the Agency. Fearful that the money, "burning" as it always does in the soldiers' pockets, would tempt his men to gamble or drink and get into mischief around the crowded post, Charlton had ordered that the troop should

march at once to the Niobrara
and wait there for his return. It
was known, of course, that many
Indian bands were out, and it
promised to be adventurous. It
was Mr. Blunt's first independent
command, too, and he felt a trifle
nervous. All went well, however,
until the morning of the second
day, when Sergeant Graham excitedly called his young commander, his face clouded with
dismay.

"Lieutenant," he cried, "Sergeant Dawson and several men
were robbed last night. The
money's clean gone!"

Blunt was out of his blanket in
an instant. "How much is missing?" he asked.

"I can't tell yet, sir—a good

deal. But that is not the worst
of it."

"What on earth could be
worse ? "

"Trumpeter Waller's gone, sir
—deserted ; taken his horse, arms,
and everything ! "

CHAPTER IV.

SUSPICIOUS CIRCUMSTANCES.

IEUTENANT BLUNT'S position on this bright July morning was most embarrassing. Personally he had known the pet trumpeter of "B" troop less than a year; for, as was said in the previous chapter, in point of actual experience on the frontier the boy was the superior of the young West Pointer, who had joined only the preceding autumn. Finding young Fred so great a favorite

among the officers and men, Mr.
Blunt was quite ready to accept
the general verdict, although his
first impression of the youngster
was that he was a trifle spoiled.
On the other hand no other man
in the troop had so favorably
impressed the new officer as the
"left principal guide," Sergeant
Dawson, whose dashing horse-
manship, fine figure and carriage,
and sharp, soldierly ways had
attracted his attention at the
first outset. Then Dawson's
manner to him was so scrupulously deferential and soldierly
on all occasions—sometimes the
old war-worn sergeants would be
a trifle supercilious with green
subalterns—that Blunt's moderate
amount of vanity was touched.

He was always glad, when his turn came round as officer of the guard, to find Sergeant Dawson on the detail, and he recalled, when he came to think over the events of his first half year with the regiment that very summer, that it was when on guard he began to imagine Fred Waller was "somewhat spoiled." Twice the boy "marched on" as orderly trumpeter when he and Dawson were on the guard detail for the day, and both times the sergeant had found fault with the musician, and had most respectfully and diplomatically, but in that semi-confidential manner which shrewd old soldiers so well know how to assume to very young subalterns, given Mr. Blunt to understand that the boy "needed looking after." Months later, when Blunt and Rayburn were discussing the probabilities of promotion, when the sergeant-major of the regiment took his discharge and there was lively competition among the soldiers for this, the finest non-commissioned post in the regiment, Blunt warmly advocated Dawson's claim. "He is the nattiest sergeant in the whole command," he said, "and the smartest one I know."

"Oh, yes!" answered Rayburn with a certain superiority of manner and a quiet sarcasm that provoked the junior officer; "there's no question about Dawson's smartness. One after another every 'plebe' in the regiment starts in with the same enthusiasm about Dawson. I had it myself about eight years ago. But the trouble with him is he isn't a stayer; he can't stand prosperity."

But Blunt preferred to hold to his own views and his faith in the second sergeant of the troop. And so it happened that on this eventful morning he sent Sergeant Graham at once to investigate as to the amounts stolen during the night, and directed that Sergeant Dawson, who was in command of the herd and. picket guard, should come to him immediately.

The sun was just rising above the low treeless ridges on the horizon as the lieutenant stood erect and looked about him. Close at hand the Niobrara — "the Running Water" — was brawling over its stony shallows, and the smoke of tiny cook-fires was floating upward into the keen, crisp, morning air. Northward the slopes were bare and treeless, too, but closely carpeted with the dense growth of buffalo grass. Only a few yards out from the bivouac, hoppled and sidelined, the troop horses were cropping the still juicy herbage, and three or four soldiers, carbine in hand and garbed in their light-blue overcoats, were posted well out beyond the herd on every side, watching the valley far and near for any signs of Indian coming. Below the bivouac, and further from the Laramie road, was an old log hut, once used as a ranch and "bar" for thirsty souls traversing the well-worn way to the reservation ; but the tide of travel had first shifted to the Sidney route, and then been stemmed entirely, so far as the line to or near the agencies was concerned, and the proprietor had taken himself and his fiery poison to better-paying fields. Far away to the southwest the blue cone of Laramie Peak stood boldly against the sky. Nearer at hand, though a day's ride away, old Rawhide Butte rose sturdily from the midst of surrounding prairie slopes. Upstream, among some sparse cottonwood, a bit of ruddy color among the branches

caught the lieutenant's quick eye.
Some Indian brave, wrapped in
his blanket, had been laid to rest
there out of reach of the snarl-
ing coyotes, one of whom could
be dimly discerned slinking away
under the bank, just out of easy
rifle range.

Off to the south lay the same
bold, barren, desolate-looking ex-
panse of rolling prairie. Blunt
could not suppress a shudder as
he thought of the terrible risk the
boy had run in his mad break for
the settlements beyond the Platte.
Of course he could go nowhere
else. North, east, and west, all
was Indian land, and no lone
white man could live there. Of
course he was making for the
cattle ranges and settlements in

Nebraska. Such at least were the lieutenant's theories. He had spent only one year on the frontier, but had been there long enough to know that among the cowboys, ranchmen, and especially among the " riff-raff " ever hanging about the small towns and settlements, a deserter from the army was apt to be welcomed and protected, if he had money, arms, or a good horse. Once plundered of all he possessed, the luckless fellow might then be turned over to the nearest post and the authorized reward of thirty dollars claimed for his apprehension ; but if well armed and sober, the deserter had little trouble in making his way through the toughest mining camps and settlements.

CHAPTER V.

TRAILING THE TRAITOR.

RED Waller knew all the Valley of the North Platte as well as he did the trails around Sanders and Red buttes, and if he could succeed in eluding the Indian war parties, he would have no difficulty in fording the river, or swimming if necessary; and, with the start he must have had, his light weight, and powerful horse, it would be next to impossible to catch him, even if they could follow his trail. Besides,

were they not ordered to remain
at the Niobrara until Charlton's return? The more Mr.
Blunt thought of the matter
the more worried and perplexed
he became. Anywhere else he
might have sent a sergeant with a
couple of men in pursuit, but here
it would be exposing them to
almost certain death. It was
some minutes before Sergeant
Dawson came in answer to the
summons. Blunt could see the
troopers gathered about the first
sergeant, excitedly discussing the
affair and bemoaning their indi-
vidual losses. Graham was noting the amounts on a slip of
paper, and his fine face was pale
with distress. " Is that all now,
men ?" he asked as he completed

the list, then sharply turned away, and once more approached his young commander.

"Lieutenant," he said, halting and raising his hand in salute, "it isn't quite so bad as I feared, but bad enough. Sergeant Farron, Corporal Watts, and I are the principal losers, besides Sergeant Dawson. Three of the men who went into the Agency on pass just after we were paid had left most of their money with me, and that is gone. I had it with my own in the flat wallet I always carried in the inside pocket of my hunting-shirt. You can see, sir, how it was done," and the sergeant displayed a long clean cut through the Indian tanned buckskin. "It took a sharp knife and a light hand to do that, for I'm not a heavy sleeper. Farron, Watts, and I were sleeping side by side just over there on the bank, and they heard nothing all the night. But will the lieutenant look at this handkerchief, sir? Is it chloroformed? I feel dull and heavy, as though I had been drugged. He couldn't have got it from me any other way."

Blunt took the bandanna and sniffed it cautiously, and then turned it over and curiously inspected it, There was certainly an odor of chloroform about it— a strong odor.

"Whose is this?" he asked. "I do not remember seeing any of the men wearing one like this."

"None of them own it, sir. I've

asked the whole party but Sergeant Dawson and the men on guard. They have these cheap red things for sale at the store there at the Red Cloud Agency, but none of the troop have I ever seen wearing them; they are too small for neck handkerchiefs. Dawson is out yet, trying to locate the trail. I've sent Robbins for him," and the sergeant looked anxiously away southward, searching the prairie with a world of pain and trouble in his eyes.

"What could possibly have induced the boy to turn scoundrel all at once?" asked the lieutenant. "It will break his old father's heart."

"I can't account for it, sir. He has been as honest and square as a

boy could be ever since his enlistment ; but the men tell me that he
has been spending a good deal of
time over in the post whenever we
camped there, and I am afraid,
from what Donovan says, that he
has been gambling with the young
fellows at the band quarters.
There's a hard lot in there, I'm
told ; and the old hands encourage
the boys to get all they can out of
strangers, and then they turn to
and fleece the boys. It is about
four hundred dollars he has taken.
A man knows that will last but a
little while on the frontier, but to
a boy it seems a big pile."

Then, rapidly approaching, the
bounding hoofs of a troop horse
were heard. Blunt eagerly turned
and saw Sergeant Dawson gallop-

ing toward them down the north bank. Reining in so suddenly as almost to throw his panting bay. upon his haunches, he vaulted lightly to the ground and stood before the lieutenant, his face beaded with sweat and his eyes glaring.

" Which way has he gone? could you tell?"

" Yes, sir, I trailed him out across the prairie yonder for three hundred yards or so. Then he took the Laramie road, and there the hoof tracks are all confused; but I knew he would never keep that line very long, and I'm almost certain I found the place where he turned off—a mile beyond the ford and well over the bluffs."

" Turned south toward the Sidney route?"

"Yes, sir, as though he was going to skirt the road a while, then make for Scott's Bluffs, keeping well west of the Sidney stage route. If he got on that he'd be likely to meet Captain Forrest's troop, sir."

"But you were in charge of the guard, sergeant. How came it that your sentries and you could let a man slip out with his horse and everything? The night was still, and they ought to have heard, even if they couldn't see."

"It was dark as pitch, lieutenant; the new moon was down before eleven o'clock; and as for hearing, the horses were uneasy and stamping or snorting all the while from midnight until two o'clock. Either they sniffed Indians, or the coyotes startled them.

Then, the stream makes such a noise over the rocks, sir ; and the lieutenant will remember we had no sentries out across the stream. The Indians couldn't stampede the herd from that direction."

" But how could he get his horse out from the herd without——"

" It wasn't there, sir," broke in the trooper, eager to defend himself against the imputation of carelessness or neglect. "Sergeant Graham will bear me out, sir, that Trumpeter Waller has been allowed to lariat his horse close by where he slept, and sometimes he'd loop the lariat by a light cord to his wrist. The captain allowed it, sir, and I supposed that the lieutenant would not care to change the captain's orders. Last night he slept, or rather made down his blanket and drove his picket-pin at the lower edge of the bivouac, sir, down there by that point; and Private Donovan tells me he moved still further down after dark. We could hear his horse whinnying a while—he didn't like being so far from the others. It's my belief, sir, he waited until all was quiet, and took some time when I was out on the prairie visiting the sentries to slip up the bank to where Sergeant Graham was sleeping, make his haul of the money, and then ride for all that he was worth as soon as he had got beyond earshot. It was easy enough to slip away through the stream without being heard."

"He has left his saddle-bags, blanket, and everything that was heavy, except his arms, behind him," said Graham moodily.

"And you really think that he has stolen the money and is trying to escape?" questioned the lieutenant.

"Indeed, sir," answered Dawson almost tearfully, "I don't know what to think. I hate to believe it of the boy we were all so fond of, though I used to plague him sometimes, just in fun—but I don't know what else to think. The men say that he has been a little wild at times, since he got from under the old man's care. But I don't know, sir; I wouldn't be apt to know what was going on in the barrack there at Robinson."

CHAPTER VI.

CONCLUSIVE EVIDENCE.

BLUNT turned sorrowfully away and began to pace slowly up and down the bank. Near at hand over a little camp-fire his coffee pot was bubbling and hissing enticingly, but even the aroma of his accustomed morning beverage failed to attract him. What was he to do? What could he do? Ordered to remain there to escort the captain safely to Red Cloud, on his return from the court, it was impossible to pursue.

Equally unwise would it be to send a small squad. Waller had taken his life in his hands when he rode away through the night, but he could cross the Rawhide and be in comparative safety, so far as the Indian attack was concerned, by sunrise of this day. Now that daylight had come, Blunt well knew that every stretch of prairie from the Platte to the White River would be thoroughly searched by keen and eager eyes, and death would be the very least that any small party of whites could expect. He knew perfectly well that already he and his little troop were being closely scrutinized from the distant ridges. Had he not seen in the tepees of the Cheyennes, but the week

before, as many as three pairs of
binocular field-glasses? and had
not Colonel Randall told him
they knew their use and value
as well as anyone? If there was
only some way of getting word
to Captain Charlton at Laramie.
There ran the single wire of the
military telegraph, but there was
neither office nor station nearer
than Red Cloud Agency. No
man in the troop would thank him
for being ordered to go either
way with dispatches, though he
knew the order would be obeyed.
Silently and gloomily, instead of
with their usual cheery alacrity,
the men had got to work with
their curry-combs and brushes and
were touching up their horses
while waiting for their own break-.

fast; and presently · Blunt's
orderly came forward, holding a
tin cup of steaming coffee.   ·

"Won't the lieutenant drink a
little of this, sir, and try a bite of
bacon? There isn't much appe-
tite in the troop this morning, sir,
but it aint so much because the
money's gone. I've known the old
sergeant and the boy nigh unto
ten years now, sir, an' I never
thought it would come to this."

Blunt thanked the soldier and
sat down at the edge of the rush-
ing stream, sipping his coffee and
trying to think what to do. The
drink warmed his blood and
cheered him up a trifle. Order-
ing his horse to be saddled, he
mounted and, taking his rifle, rode
through the Niobrara and out

upon the open prairie on the other side. It was not long before he found the hoof-tracks made the night before, and, without knowing why, he slowly followed them out toward the low ridge at the south-west. For ten minutes he went at a quiet walk and with downward-searching eyes as he reached the road, striving to decide which hoof-prints were made by Waller's horse.

Suddenly, back at camp he heard the ringing report of a cavalry carbine borne on the rising breeze, and, whirling about, saw that they were signaling to him. Putting spurs to his steed he galloped full tilt for the ford, and then for the first time saw the cause of the excitement. Far up on the opposite slope, and jogging

easily down toward the troop, came
an Indian pony and an Indian
rider, but not in war-paint and
feathers. As Mr. Blunt plunged
through the stream he recognized
the young half-breed scout known
to all of the soldiers as "Little
Bat," and Bat, without a word, rode
up and handed him a letter. It
was from the commanding officer
at Fort Robinson, and very much
to the point. It read somewhat
as follows :

"Captain Charlton telegraphs
that he will be detained several
days. Meantime you are needed
here, as the Indians are again
quitting the reservations in large
numbers. Move immediately upon receipt of this."

JOGGING ALONG AT AN EASY PACE.

That evening therefore the little troop once more rode down the valley of the White River, the "Smoking Earth" as the Indians called it, and by sunset were camped at Red Cloud. In much distress of mind Mr. Blunt called upon the commanding officer to tell him of the disappearance of the money and his trumpeter, and to ask the colonel's advice as to the proper course for him to pursue. It was agreed that telegrams should be sent at once to the captain at Fort Laramie and to the commanding officer at Sidney barracks on the railway, notifying them of the crime and the desertion. Blunt begged for a moment's delay until he could hear from Sergeant Graham, whom he had sent to make certain investigations, and long before tattoo the sergeant came—and with him the hospital steward.

"Lieutenant, the store-keeper says he sold just such a handkerchief as that to Trumpeter Waller last week, and the steward can tell about the chloroform."

Both officers looked inquiringly at the steward.

"Yes, sir, it was pay day that young Waller handed me a penciled note from Sergeant Graham, saying that he had a bad toothache and asking for a little chloroform, and I gave it to him."

"I never wrote such a note, sir, and never sent him on such a message," said Graham.

CHAPTER VII.

TELEGRAPHIC DISPATCHES.

BAD news travels fast. Captain Charlton at Fort Laramie was stunned by the tidings flashed to him by telegraph from Red Cloud. Despite the array of damaging evidence, he could not bring himself to believe that Fred Waller was a thief: but he was sore at heart when he thought of the misery and sorrow the news must bring to the dear ones at his army home—above all to the proud old sergeant, whose life seemed almost bound up in the boy. Well knowing that it could only be a day or two before the story would make its way to the posts along the railroad, and would reach Sanders, doubtless, in a more exaggerated form, the captain decided to warn his wife at once, and by the stage leaving that very night a letter went in to Cheyenne, and thence by train over the great "divide" of the Rockies to Fort Sanders, giving to Mrs. Charlton all particulars thus far received, but charging her to say nothing until further tidings.

"I cannot believe it [wrote he], and am going at once to join the troop and make full investigation. Meantime I have written by the same mail to Major Edwards, who commands at Sidney barracks, to make every effort to trace the boy, should he have come south of the Platte; and you must be sure to see, when the news reaches Sanders, that the sergeant is assured of my disbelief in the whole story, and of my determination that Fred shall have justice done him. It will be several days before you can hear from me again."

And the news reached Sanders, as he feared, all too soon. Telegraph offices "leaked" on the frontier in those days. The operators at the military stations were all enlisted men, who were not bound by the regulations of the

Western Union, and who could
not keep to themselves every item
of personal interest. The Sidney
office wired mysterious inquiries
to Sanders; Sanders insisted on
knowing what it meant, and presently Laramie, Sanders, Sidney,
Russell, Red Cloud, and even Chug
Water were clicking away in con-
fidential discussion over the ex-
traordinary theft and flight. And
Mrs. Charlton's letter came none
too early to save old Waller from
despair. It was a woman, a gab-
bling laundress, who first told him
of the rumor, and Mrs. Charlton
saw him hastening to the telegraph office just as she had
finished reading the letter.

"Mr. Nelson, quick!" she called
to a young officer just passing the

gate. "Stop Sergeant Waller at once. Don't let him go to the office. Make him come here to me. He will hear and obey you."

And Mr. Nelson touched his cap, leaped lightly across the acequia, and his powerful young voice was heard thundering, "Sergeant Waller!" in peremptory tones across the parade. "Sergeant Waller!" echoed a half dozen voices as the loungers on barrack porches took up the cry, "Lieutenant Nelson wants you!" and the soldier instinct prevailed, the old man turned and hastened toward the officers' quarters.

"What is it, Mrs. Charlton," asked Nelson. "Has there been another fight? Is Fred killed? It will break the old man's heart."

"Oh, Mr. Nelson! I can't tell you about it yet!" she almost wailed. "There's bad news, and I'm afraid the old man has heard it. Stay here, near me a moment, can you? Oh, look at his face! Look at his face! He has heard."

White, livid, trembling from head to foot, the old soldier hurried toward the young officer and dumbly raised his hand in the mechanical salute.

"It is Mrs. Charlton who wants you, sergeant," said Mr. Nelson kindly. "Go to her," and without a word the veteran passed in at the gate.

She held forth her hand, her eyes brimming with tears. Instinctively he halted, the old respect and reverence for "captain's

HE RAISED HIS HANDS AND PRESSED THEM TO HIS EYES.

lady " checking the wild torrent of
grief and anxiety, but she caught
him by the arm and led him wondering and submissive, yet overwhelmed with cruel dread, into her
cool and darkened parlor. There,
with wild, imploring eyes, the old
man half stretched forth two
palsied hands, his forage cap fall-
ing unheaded to the floor, his
whole frame shaking.

"Don't give way, sergeant;
don't believe it!" she cried, and at
her first words a look as of horror
came into the stricken old face,
and the hands clasped together in
piteous appeal. "Listen to what
the captain says. His letter has
just come, and I was sure, when I
saw you, that someone had told
you the rumor. Captain Charl-

ton will not believe a word of it.
He was at Laramie on court-martial or it would not have happened. He has hurried back to
Red Cloud to investigate, and he
declares that Fred •shall have
justice done him. I'll never believe it—never! Why, we would
trust him with anything we
owned."

"I—I thank the captain. I
thank Mrs. Charlton," he brokenly
replied. "It's stunned like I am."
He raised his hands and pressed
them against his eyes, and one of
them was lowered suddenly, feebly
groping for support. She seized
his arm and strove to lead him to
a sofa. "You must sit down,
sergeant," she said.

"No, ma'am, no!" he protested,

straightening himself with a violent effort. " Now, may I hear what it is they say against my boy, ma'am ? I want every word. Don't be afraid, ma'am, I can bear it."

Then, with infinite sympathy and pity, she told him, softening every detail, suggesting an explanation for every circumstance that pointed to his guilt ; and all the time the old man stood there, his eyes, filled with dumb anguish, fixed upon her face, his hands clasped together as though in entreaty, his fingers twitching nervously. At every new and damaging detail, condone or explain it though she would, he shuddered as though smitten with a sharp, painful spasm ; but when

it came to Fred's midnight disappearance—horse, arms, and all—in
the heart of the Indian country,
stealing away from his comrades
in the shadow of disgrace and
crime, the old man groaned aloud
and buried his face in his hands.
Some time he stood there, reeling,
yet resisting her efforts to draw
him to a seat. She pleaded with
him hurriedly, impulsively, yet he
seemed not to hear. At last with
one long shivering sigh, he suddenly straightened up and faced
her. His hands fell by his side,
He cleared his throat and strove
to speak :

"You've been good to me,
ma'am—so good"—and here he
choked, and for a moment could
not go on—"and to my boy"—at

last he finished, with impulsive
rush of words. "I know how
they're sometimes tempted. I
know how, more than once, the
little fellow would be led away by
the roughs in the troop, just to
worry me; but he never hid a
thing from me, ma'am, never; and
if he's in trouble now he would
tell me the whole truth, even if
it broke us both down. I'll not
believe it till I see him, ma'am;
but I must go—I must go until I
find my boy."

Blinded with tears, Mrs. Charlton could hardly see the swaying,
grief-bowed old soldier as he left
the house; but Nelson was waiting close at hand, and stepped forward and took his place by the
sergeant's side.

"I don't know what the trouble is," he said, "but I'm going as far as the headquarters with you, and if there is anything on earth I can do to help you, do not fail to tell me."

That night, with a week's furlough and a letter from his post commander to Major Edwards at Sidney, old Sergeant Waller was jolting eastward in the caboose of a freight train.

CHAPTER VIII.

LOYAL FRIENDS.

T was on Friday morning, at daybreak, that the desertion of Trumpeter Waller was reported to Lieutenant Blunt. It was Friday night that the telegrams were sent to Laramie and that Charlton's letter left by stage. It was Saturday afternoon just before parade that the mail was distributed at Fort Sanders ; and that very evening, before Major Edwards had received and had time to read his letter from the

West, the sergeant had started on his long and fatiguing journey. All night long in sleepless misery he sat in a corner of the caboose, occasionally rising and tramping unsteadily to and fro. At Cheyenne a delay of half an hour occurred, and he left the train and paced restlessly up and down the platform under the freight sheds. He dared not go down to the lighted offices and the crowded passenger station just below him. It seemed as though everyone knew of Fred's story by this time. He could see the gleam of forage-cap ornaments and the glint of army buttons among the people at the dépot, and knew there were several officers and soldiers there. Never before had he known what it was to shrink from facing any man on earth ; but to-night, though he almost starved for further news from his boy, he could not bring himself to meet them and ask.

Along toward morning, at Pine Bluffs, a herdsman got aboard, and what he had to say was of startling interest. Hitherto the Indian war parties had kept well to the north of the Platte, "but" said he, "ever since Friday the Sidney road has been swarming with them—both sides of the river —and they are killing everything white they can lay their hands on."

"My God!" thought Waller, "and Fred must be in the very midst of them. Better so," he added, "if indeed he can be guilty." The herder had evidently been sorely frightened by all he heard, and he was hurrying to Sidney to join a party of cattlemen who were camping there. He had been drinking too, and took more and more as the night wore on, and became maudlin in his talk. It was nine o'clock on Sunday morning when they reached Sidney station, and the first thing that old Waller saw was a strong concord wagon with a four-mule team and an army driver. Two infantry soldiers with their rifles and girt with cartridge-belts were standing close at hand. Two officers were stowing their rifles inside the wagon, and an orderly was strapping the tarpaulin over the light luggage in the

"boot." One of the officers the
sergeant knew instantly—an aid-
de-camp of the commanding
general. The other was older in
years and bore on his cap the
insignia of the staff. The younger
officer saw him before he could
step into the office, and Sergeant
Waller knew it—knew too, with
the quickness of thought, that he
had heard of Fred's disappearance
and presumable crime. He could
have shrunk from meeting his su-
periors in the shadow of this bitter
sorrow and disgrace. Even while
he could not accept the belief that
his boy was actually a deserter
and a thief, he knew full well what
other men must think. But Captain Cross was a cavalryman himself, and had known old Waller

for years. He dropped his rifle, came straight forward, and took him by the hand.

" Sergeant, I don't believe it of your boy ; I've known his father too long," was all he said, as he pressed the veteran's hand. Poor old Waller, worn with anguish, long vigil, and utter lack of food of any kind, was now so weak that he could only, with the utmost difficulty, choke back the sobs that shook his frame. Speak he dare not ; he would have broken down. Cross led him to the lunch room at the station and made him swallow a cup of coffee, then gently questioned him as to what he knew.

" We go at once to Red Cloud —Colonel Gaines and I — and

maybe on the road I shall hear something of him. Sergeant, rest assured your son shall have fair play," said the aid-de-camp, as he was about to turn away.

"But, captain—I beg pardon, sir," broke in Waller hurriedly, in almost the first words he had spoken. "Where is your escort? Surely you won't take this route without one?"

"There isn't a trooper at Sidney, sergeant. We have a couple of infantrymen in the wagon and another on a mule. That's the best we can do, and we've got no time to spare. We must be at Red Cloud to-morrow, and this is the shortest line."

"But, sir, haven't you heard? The Sioux are out in force and

all along the road, both above
and below the Platte. There's a
herder on the train who told us.
He got aboard at Pine Bluffs
this morning."

" I can hardly believe that,"
answered Cross. " Captain Forrest with the Grays is scouting
south of Red Cloud. Captain
Wallace was ordered to watch the
fords along the Platte on this
line ; Captain Charlton is out—
or at least the whole troop has
been, and there are three more.
Surely Major Edwards would
know over at the barracks, if the
Indians were anywhere between
us and the river,—we'll get an
escort from Captain Wallace the
other side,—but he has not heard
a word."

"But I beg the captain to hear what the man says, sir," urged Sergeant Waller. "He's been drinking, but he tells the same story, practically, that he told us when he got aboard. Let me find him, sir."

And find him he did, even more maudlin and thick-tongued by this time, and evidently determined to make the most of his dramatic story for the benefit of the two officers and swarm of interested lookers-on. He only succeeded in inspiring the colonel with mingled incredulity and disgust.

"I don't believe a word of it," he said to Captain Cross. "And we are losing valuable time. We must start at once."

An hour later this peaceful
Sabbath morning, the sergeant
stood, cap in hand, before Major
Edwards on the veranda. of his
pleasant quarters. Two pretty
children were playing with a big,
shaggy, lazy staghound, pulling
his ears and tormenting him in
various ways ; a pleasant-faced lady
came forth, sunshade and prayer
book in hand, and at sight of
her the little ones reluctantly rose
and bade good-by to their four-
footed friend, and the party
started slowly away across the
green parade to the post chapel,
nodding and smiling to the spruce
orderly, who stood respectfully
aside to let them pass. Mrs.
Edwards glanced quickly and
sympathetically into the ser-

geant's sad face as he stood there
before her husband's easy-chair.
She knew well what it all meant,
but there was nothing for her to
say. Small parties of infantry
officers and of ladies and children
joined them on the way to the
humble wooden sanctuary; the
soft notes of the bugle were
sounding church call; a warm
gentle breeze from the southern
plains stirred the folds of the big
flag; the sunshine was joyous and
brilliant, and all spoke of peace,
order, and contentment. Yet
there stood Waller with almost
bursting heart; and yonder, only
a few miles across the grassy
ridge to the north, rode that little
party of officers and men to almost certain death.

The major looked up as he finished reading the letter placed in his hands.

"I have no words to tell you of my sympathy and sorrow, sergeant. Of course you know my plain duty in the matter. The sheriff has been notified, and two of his deputies already have gone out to search. He would hardly be mad enough to come anywhere near us, if guilty. But if he is taken he will be held here under my charge, and I will see that you have every proper opportunity of visiting him. The adjutant tells me you had heard something of the Indians being south of the Platte. What was it?"

"A man who boarded our train at the Bluffs, sir. He claimed to

have had to ride hard for his life
yesterday afternoon, and that
there were scores of the Sioux
this side of the river. I took him
to Colonel Gaines and Captain
Cross, sir; but the man had been
drinking so much that they dis-
trusted him entirely. They left
the station before I started for the
barracks, sir."

The major sat thoughtfully
gazing out across the parade a
moment; then answered:

"We have had no rumors of
anything of the kind, and they
would be almost sure to come this
way to us, if anyone heard of such
stories. There are no settlers
along the road, after leaving the
springs, out here until you reach
the Platte. I can hardly believe

it, but we'll see what can be got from the man when he sobers up. Now · the sergeant-major will go with you to the quarters, and I will see you later in the day."

But later in the day that promise was forgotten in an excitement of far greater magnitude.

CHAPTER IX.

LURKING FOES.

CHURCH was over. The bugler had just sounded mess call, and the soldiers in their neat "undress" uniform were just going in to dinner, when a man on a "cow pony"—one of those wiry, active little steeds so much in use around the cattle-herd—came full speed into the garrison and threw himself from the saddle at Major Edwards' gate. It was the telegraph operator at the railway station. In his hands were two brown envelopes, and Major Edwards, as he stepped forward to meet him, saw in his face the tell-tale look of a bearer of bad news.

"I've no idea whose horse that is, major. There were a half dozen of 'em in front of a saloon there in town, and I jumped on the first I saw. These have just come—one from Laramie, one from Omaha. I dropped everything at the office to fetch them to you."

Edwards tore open first one and then the other. The first read :

"Couriers in front of Captain Wallace report large war parties along the Platte, and some across, raiding the Sidney road. Four

teamsters killed, scalped, and muti-
lated three miles south of river.
Bodies found. Warn back everybody attempting to go that way."

The second was from the office
of the department commander
himself :

" Indians in force south of
Platte, on Sidney road. If Colonel Gaines and Captain Cross
have started, send couriers at once
to recall them."

The major's face was dark with
dismay.

"They have been gone nearly
four hours," he exclaimed. "Even
if I had swift riders ready, who
could catch them in time?"

"I've been a trooper all my life, sir," came sudden answer. "Give me a horse and carbine and let me go."

The major might have known 'twas Sergeant Waller.

True to his word, and arranging with the officers of the court-martial to return in case his further testimony was required, Captain Charlton set forth at daybreak on Saturday, intending to push straight through to Red Cloud as fast as mules could drag or horses bear him. To the Niobrara crossing the road was hard and smooth, when once they cleared the sandy wastes of the Platte bottom. He had a capital team, a light ambulance, and a

little squad of seasoned troopers
to go with him as escort. It was
a drive of nearly ninety miles, but
he proposed resting his animals
an hour at the Niobrara, another
hour at sunset; feeding and water-
ing carefully each time, and so
keeping on to the old Agency
until he reached his troop late at
night.

No danger was to be appre-
hended until the party got beyond
the Rawhide, and not very much
until they were across the Niobrara, but Charlton and his half
a dozen troopers had been over
each inch of the ground time and
again, and very little did they
dread the Sioux.

After midday the little party
had halted close beside the spot

where Blunt's detachment had made their bivouac so short a time before. Here were the ashes of their cook-fires and the countless hoof-prints of the horses. Here, too, was the trail in double file, leading away northward across the prairie—a short cut to the Red Cloud road. Charlton followed it with his keen eyes, and noted with a smile how straight a line its young leader must have made for the "dip" in the grassy ridge a mile away, through which ran the hard, beaten track. Blunt prided himself on these little points of soldiership, as the captain well remembered, and when charged with guiding at the head of a column, was pretty sure to fix his eyes on

some distant landmark and steer
for that, with little regard for what
might be going on at the rear.

The ambulance mules, tethered
about the tongue, were busily
crunching their liberal measure of
oats. Each cavalry horse, too,
buried his nose deep in the shimmering pile his rider had carefully
poured for him upon the dry side
of the saddle-blanket. The men
were contentedly eating their hard-
tack and bacon and drinking their
coffee from huge tin cups with the
relish of old frontiersmen. One
trooper, a few yards away out on
the prairie, kept vigilant watch.
Pondering deeply over the strange
and unaccountable charge that
had been laid at his young
trumpeter's door, the captain was

slowly pacing down the bank, puffing away at the briar root pipe that was the constant companion of his scouting days. Suddenly he heard the sentry call, and, turning, saw him pointing to the ground at his feet.

" What is it, Horton ? " he asked, going over toward him.

" Pony tracks, sir. The Indians have been nosing around here since our men left."

There were the prints of some half a dozen little unshod hoofs dotting the sandy hollows in the low ground near the stream, and easily traceable among the clumps of buffalo grass beyond. Charlton could see where they had gathered in one spot, as though their riders were then in consultation, and then scattered once more along the bank. Two hundred yards away stood the lonely log cabin, all that was left of what had been the ranch, and following the trail, the captain presently found himself nearing it. Two tracks seemed to lead straight thither, and before he reached it were joined by several more. Close to the abandoned hut the ground was worn smooth and hard ; yet in the hollows were accumulations of dust blown from the roadway up the stream. Around here the pony tracks were thick, and just within the gaping doorway were footprints in the dust—some of spurred bootheels and broad soles, one still more recent of Sioux moccasins. Through the solid log

walls two small square windows
had been cut and narrow slits for
rifles, in the days when the occu-
pants had frequent occasion to
defend their prairie castle. The
opening to the subterranean
"keep" was yawning under the
eastern wall, its wooden cover
having long since been broken up
for fuel. Charlton stood for a
moment within the blackened and
dusty doorway, and glanced curiously around him.

Except for the new footprints it
looked very much as it did when
he had first taken occasion to in-
spect the interior, earlier in the
summer. There was nothing left
that anyone could carry away, and
he wondered why the Indians
should have troubled themselves

to dismount and prowl about. An
Indian hates a house on general
principles, and enters one only
when he expects to make something by it. Those recent boot-
prints, nearly effaced by the moccasins, were doubtless those of
some of Blunt's party. Curiosity
had prompted some time-killing
trooper to stroll out here and take
a look at the place. The sunshine streaming in at the open
doorway made a brilliant oblong
square upon the earthen floor and
lighted up the grimy interior.
The steps cut down to the dark
"dugout" were crumbling away,
and it was impossible to see more
than a few feet into the passage
leading to the underground for-
tress, where as a final resort in an

Indian siege the little garrison could take refuge. A lantern or a candle would show the way, but Charlton had neither. Taking out his match-case, however, he bent down, struck a light, and peered in. Somebody had done the same thing within the last day or two, for there were the stub ends of two matches just like his in the dust at the bottom of the steps, and there, too—yes, he lighted another match and studied it carefully—there was the print of cavalry boots going in and coming out again. Whoever was his predecessor, he had more curiosity than the captain. Charlton had seen prairie "dugout" forts before, and did not care to waste time now.

CHAPTER X.

RETURNING to the open sunshine he made the circuit of the house, and on the north side stopped and studied with an interest he had not felt before. A stout post was still standing on that side, and to the post a cavalry horse had been tethered within two days, and stood there long enough to paw and trample the gravel all around it. Charlton was cavalryman enough to read in every sign

113

that the steed had been most un-
willingly detained. In evident
impatience he had twisted twice
and again around that stubborn
bullet-scarred stump, and the troop
commander could almost see him,
pawing vigorously, tugging at
his "halter-shank," and plunging
about his hated but relentless
jailer, and neighing loudly in hopes
of calling back his departing
friends. Charlton felt sure that,
as the troop rode away, some one
of the men had remained here
some little time.

A hundred yards across the
prairie was the "double file" trail
of the detachment on its straight
line for the ridge, and here, only a
little distance out, were the hoof-
prints of a troop horse both com-

ing and going. Even more interested now, the captain went
some distance out across the
prairie, and still he found them.
Leaving the hut and following to
overtake the troop, the horse had
instantly taken the gallop; the
prints settled that. But what
struck Captain Charlton as strange
was that the other tracks, those
which were made by the same
horse in coming to the hut, were
still to be found far out toward the
northeast. It was evident, then,
that the rider had not turned back
from the command until it had
marched some distance from the
Niobrara; that he had not gone
back to the bank where they had
been in camp, as would have been
the case had he lost or left some-

thing behind, but had come here to this abandoned hovel south-east of the trail. Now, what did that mean ? One other thing the captain did not fail to note ; that horse had cast a shoe.

Late as it was when he reached the camp on White River that night—after midnight, as it proved—Charlton found his young lieutenant up, and anxiously awaiting him. When the horses had all been cared for, and the two officers were alone near their tents, almost the first question asked by the captain was :

"Did you give any man permission to ride back after you left the Niobrara Friday morning ?

"No, sir," answered Blunt in some surprise. "No one asked,

and every man was in his place when we made our first halt."

Immediately after reveille on Sunday morning, a good hour before the sun was high enough to peep over the tall white crags to the east of the little camp, the two officers were out at the line, superintending the grooming of the horses. Fifty men were now present for duty, and fifty active steeds were tethered there at the picket rope, nipping at each other's noses or nibbling at the rope itself, and pricking up their ears as the captain stopped to pat or to speak to one after another of his pets. Always particularly careful of his horses, Captain Charlton on this bright sunshiny morning was noting especially the condition of their feet. Every one of those two hundred hoofs were keenly scrutinized as he passed along the line. But there was nothing un-usual in this—he never let a week go by without it.

" You seem to have had a num-ber reshod within the last few hours, sergeant," he said to Graham, as he stopped at the end of the line.

" Yes, sir, I looked them all over yesterday morning. Every shoe is snug and ready now, in case we have to go out. Seven horses were reshod yesterday, and over twenty had the old shoes tacked on."

Grooming over, each trooper vaulted on to the bare back of his horse and rode in orderly

column down to the running
stream, and still Charlton stood
there, silently watching his men
and noting the condition of their
steeds. Blunt was bustling about
his duties, every now and then
looking over at his soldierly
captain. Something told him
that the troop commander had
made a discovery or two that
had set him to thinking. He
was even more silent than
usual.

At seven o'clock, after a re-
freshing dip in a pool under the
willows close at hand, the two
officers were seated on their
camp-stools and breakfasting at
the lid of the mess chest. Over
among the brown buildings of
the post, half a mile away, the

bugles were sounding mess call
and the infantry people were
waking up to the duties of the
day. Down the valley, still
farther to the east, the smoke
was curling from the tiny fires
among the Indian tepees, and
scores of ponies were grazing
out along the slopes, watched
by little urchins in picturesque
but dirty tatters. All was very
still and peaceful. Even the
hulking squaws and old men
loafing about the Agency store-
houses were silent, and patiently
waiting for the coming of the
clerk with his keys of office.
One or two young braves rode
by the camp, shrouded in their
dark-blue blankets, and appar-
ently careless of any change in

the condition of affairs, yet never failing to note that there were fifty horses and soldiers ready for duty there in camp.

Their breakfast finished, Charlton said that he must go at once to the office of the post commander over in garrison, and that he might be detained some hours. "It will be well to keep the men here, Blunt, for we may be needed any moment."

And yet, as he was riding away with his orderly, Charlton stopped to listen to what Sergeant Graham had to say.

"Sergeant Dawson and Private Donovan wanted particularly to go over to the post for a few hours this morning, and so did some of the others, but I told

them that the captain's orders
were we should all stay at camp,
we were almost sure to be wanted.
They were all satisfied, sir, but
Dawson and Donovan, who made
quite a point of it, and I said
I would carry their request to
the captain." And to Blunt's
surprise, as well as that of Sergeant Graham, the captain coolly
nodded.

"Very well. They've both been
doing hard work of late. Tell
them to keep their ears open for
'boots and saddles'; otherwise
they may stay until noon. After
dinner, perhaps, I will give others
a chance to turn."

Fifteen minutes later Captain
Charlton was in consultation with
the post commander, and after

guard mounting they returned to the colonel's house, where a tall infantry soldier, the provost sergeant, was awaiting him.

CHAPTER XI.

HEMMED·IN BY SAVAGE FOES.

BACK at the cavalry camp there was no little subdued chat and wonderment among the troopers. Lounging in the shade of the trees along the stream, and puffing away at their pipes, play. ing cards, as soldiers will, and poking fun at one another in rough, good-natured ways, the men were yet full of the one absorbing theme—Fred Waller's most unaccountable disappearance and the loss of so much of their hard-earned money.

".I would have bet any amount," said Corporal Wright, "that when the old man"—the captain is always the "old man" to his troops—"got back he would ride over Sergeant Dawson roughshod for letting Waller slip away on his guard; but I listened to him this morning and he talked to him just like a Dutch uncle. I tell you Dawson felt a heap better after it was over. He said the captain never blamed him at all."

Noon came, so did an orderly telling Mr. Blunt that the captain wished to see him over at the telegraph office, and to order the horses fed at once. Forty-eight big portions of oats were poured from the sacks forthwith. Dawson and Donovan were not yet back.

"Leave theirs out," said Sergeant Graham, "they'll be back presently. This means business again, and no mistake. Where's the trouble now, I wonder?"

Shall we look and see? Far to the south, far beyond the bold bluffs of the White River, far beyond the swift waters of the Niobrara,—"L'Eau qui Court" of the old French trapper,—far across the swirling flood of the North Platte, and dotting the northward slopes, swarms of naked, brilliantly painted red warriors in their long, trailing war bonnets of eagle's feathers are darting about on nimble ponies, or, crouching prone along the ridges, are eagerly watching a dust-cloud coming northward on the Sidney road.

Behind them, between them and
the Platte, are the weltering muti-
lated bodies of half a dozen
herders and teamsters, and the
smoking ruins of their big freight-
wagons. Like the tiger's taste of
blood, the savage triumph in the
death of their hapless foes has
tempted them far beyond their
accustomed limits. Knowing the
cavalry to be scouting only north
of the Platte, they have made a
wide detour and swooped around
to this danger-haunted road,
eagerly watching for the coming
of other white men, who, like the
last, should be ignorant of their
presence and too few in number
to cope with such a foe. Here
along the ridge north of the little
" Branch " of the Platte, half a

hundred young warriors crouch and wait. Farther back, equally vigilant, other bands are hiding among the breaks and ravines near the river, while their scouts keep vigilant watch for the coming of cavalry. Forrest's Grays and Wallace's Sorrels cannot be more than a day's ride away, and will be hurrying for the road the moment they know that the Indians have slipped around them. Wallace, up the Platte, has already heard.

It is three o'clock this hot, still Sunday afternoon, and they have been six hours out from Sidney, driving swiftly and steadily northward, when, as they reach the summit of a high ridge and stop to breathe their panting team,

Colonel Gaines takes a long look through his field glass. Just in front is the shallow valley of the little stream now called the "Pumpkinseed" though pumpkins were unheard-of features in the landscape of fifteen years ago.

Off to their right front, several miles away, lie the low, broad bottom lands of the Platte. Across the Pumpkinseed, a mile distant, another ridge, like the one on which they halted, only not so high ; to the westward a tumbling sea of prairie upland—all buttes, ridges, ravines, coulées—but not a living soul is anywhere in sight. Far as his practiced eye can sweep. the horizon and the broad lowlands of the Platte not a sign of living, moving object can Colonel

Gaines detect. Turning around, he trains his glass upon the tortuous road they had been following, and along which the dust is slowly settling in their wake. Something seems to attract his gaze, for he holds the binocle steadily toward the south. Naturally Captain Cross and the two soldiers follow with their eyes; the third infantryman has dismounted, and is readjusting the girths of his saddle.

"What is it?" asks Cross.

"I can't make out," is the reply, "Something is kicking up a dust there, some miles behind us. A horseman, I should say, though I've seen nobody. Wait a few minutes. He's down in a swale now, whoever it is."

Everybody turns to look and

HE TOOK A LONG LOOK THROUGH HIS GLASSES.

listen. Those were days when such a thing as a single horseman following in pursuit had a meaning that is lacking now.

Three, four minutes they wait in silence; then the colonel suddenly exclaims:

"I have him—a mere dot yet!"

Presently he lowers his glasses, and dusts the lenses with his handkerchief. His face is graver.

"Whoever that is, he is riding for all he is worth," he says. "I half believe he wants to catch us."

Another long look. Utter silence in the party. A mule in the wheel team gives an impatient shake of his entire system, and chains, tugs, and swing-bars all rattle noisily.

"Quiet there, you fool!" growls

the driver angrily, and with a
threatening sweep of his long
whip-lash. Then the silence
becomes intense again, and every
man strains his eyes over the
prairie slopes shimmering in the
heat of the July sun. Suddenly
an exclamation bursts from two
or three pairs of bearded lips.
Far away, but in plain sight in
that rare atmosphere, a speck of a
horseman darts into view over a
distant ridge, sweeps down the
slope at full gallop, and plunges
out of sight again in a low dip of
the rolling surface.

" No man rides like that unless
there is mischief abroad," mutters
Cross, as he swings out of the
wagon to the ground. " Give me
my rifle, Murray."

Then, sudden as thunderclap
from summer sky, with wild, shrill
clamor, with thunder of hoofs, and
sputter of rapid shots; with yell
and taunt and hideous war cry,
from the very ground itself, from
behind every little ridge; up from
the ravines, down from the prairie
buttes; hurling upon them in
mad, raging race, there flashes
into sight of their startled eyes a
horde of painted savages.

"The Sioux! The Sioux!"
yells the driver, as he leaps from
his box.

"Hang on to your mules!"
shouts Cross. "Down with you,
men! Fire slow! They'll veer
when they get in closer. Now!"

Bang! goes Cross' piece.
Bang! bang! the rifles of the

nearest soldiers. The mules plunge wildly, and are tangled in an instant in the traces. Over goes the wagon with a crash. Bang goes Gaines' big Springfield as he coolly spreads himself on the ground. An Indian pony stumbles and hurls his rider on the turf, and Cross gives an exultant cheer. Yet all the same he knows full well that now it is life or death. The little party is hemmed in by a host of savage foes.

CHAPTER XII.

MYSTERIOUS HOOF-PRINTS.

T was Saturday night that, from far up the Platte, the news came to Captain Wallace of the dash made by the Sioux for the Sidney road. For two days previous he had been hunting Indians upstream toward the Rawhide, and had found a perfect network of pony tracks and had had some very distant glimpses of flitting warriors. His scouts had told him that the Sioux and Cheyennes were swarming over the

country to the northwest of him,
and that none had appeared to
the east. It was his business,
therefore, to move against them,
and move he did, trusting that
Forrest and the Grays would
be alert along the southern verge
of the reservations that no formi-
dable parties could slip southward
in his absence.

But this was simply part and
parcel of the Indian scheme.
·Having lured him two days' march
away from the Sidney crossing,
these enterprising warriors kept
him occupied, while their con-
federates, making a wide detour
around Forrest, slipped across the
Platte and swooped down upon
the poor fellows with the freight
wagons. Only one of their num-

ber managed to escape, and he, madly riding westward, came upon some herdsmen who promptly joined him in his flight. They had seen the cavalry going up the north bank a day or two before, and they never drew rein until they found them. Wallace at once sent couriers westward to Fort Laramie with the news, and at break of day started down-stream with his whole troop. They had not marched five miles before they came upon the hoof-prints of a single horse, and just beyond the point where these hoofprints crossed their trail, the tracks of half a dozen Indian ponies met their eager eyes. One old sergeant, reining out of column to the right, followed the shod tracks

over to the river bank, and a lieutenant spurred out and joined him
when he signaled with his broad-
brimmed scouting hat. The rest
of the troop moved stolidly ahead.

Presently the young officer
overtook the column and reined
in beside his captain.

"Where did they go, Park?"

"Straight into the stream, sir,
and evidently to the other side.
Sergeant Brooks says 'twas a
troop horse with a light rider, and
that he had to swim across. The
river is six feet deep out there,
but it was his only way of escape.
The Indians couldn't have been
far behind, and yet they didn't
follow. Their tracks turn down
the bank on this side. Brooks is
following them now."

"Who on earth could have come through here at such a time? Why, the country has been running over with Indians!"

"That's what puzzles me, sir, but Brooks says there is no mistake. It's the cavalry shoe, of course. It's just after pay day at Robinson. Could it have been a deserter?"

"No man in his senses would have dared such a thing," is the impatient answer. "It may be some other infernal trick to get us away from our legitimate business. What we've got to do is reach that Sidney road by sunset. By Jove! if I'm court-martialed for this business, it won't surprise me." And the captain's horse evidently felt the sudden grip of the knees, for he took a sudden spurt and set most of the troop at the nerve-wearing jog-trot. Mr. Park said nothing more, but for the life of him he could not help thinking of those lone hoofprints and of that solitary rider. Who could he be?

It is time we got back to him. Only one man or boy, known to us at least, could have come that way. It was Trumpeter Fred.

Daybreak Friday had found him a few miles south of the Niobrara, and close to the Laramie road. At noon Friday he had halted at the Rawhide to rest his horse and take a bite of luncheon, but all his young soul was athrill with eagerness ; every faculty was alert. Warned of the recent presence of Indians on every side, he was yet

seeking to gain the Platte before
nightfall; cross to the south bank.
where there was comparative
safety; ride southeastward until
his horse was exhausted, picket him
where grass and water were near
at hand, sleep till dawn again, and
then push on. He must reach the
Sidney road before Sunday morning and strike it far below the
river.

But here, as he neared the valley, a sight had met his eyes which
made his young heart leap. The
banks of the Rawhide were dotted
here and there by fresh pony
tracks, and, coming from the distant ridges to the east, they had
gone in as though to water, and
then turned down toward the
Platte, the very way he wanted to

go. An hour, with his horse hidden behind him in a shallow ravine, Fred Waller was lying prone upon the ground, and peering over a ridge into the low, level wastes stretching far to the southeast, bordering the Platte to the very horizon. What most attracted his gaze was a little dust cloud, miles away downstream, into which tiny black dots were moving, with other little dots scurrying about at some distance from the main cluster. No need to tell him they were Indians.

It was some minutes before he could determine which way they were really going, but when he finally saw that they were bound down the valley, the boy's heart beat high with hope. He could

FLAT ON THE GROUND WAS PEERING OVER THE RIDGE.

venture down to the Platte as soon
as they had passed entirely out of
sight, and find some place to cross
well to the west of them. An
hour he waited and still they were
in view. Then they seemed to
disappear in a little clump of timber. He waited fifteen to twenty
minutes, and they were still there.
Then it suddenly dawned upon
him that the whole band were
resting in the shade while their
scouts searched the neighborhood.
He was five or six miles from the
river, and every inch of ground in
front was open. He knew well
that their eyes were keener than
his, and should he make a dash for
it they would certainly see and
give chase. What he could not
detect, and did not dream of, was

that miles still further away down the Platte another dust cloud was slowly advancing—Wallace's troop coming upstream—and their scouts were watching that.

At last, after another hour of anxiety, he determined to slip away westward, go up the Rawhide a few miles until he could gain the shelter of some low-lying ridges, crossing the stream, and making a wide circuit, sweep around to the Platte. He might still reach it before dark and find a ford, or at least a place to swim across ; he could trust " Big Jim " for that. But even as he would have put this plan in execution, he saw to his dismay a new move among the warriors. Four little dots came riding from the timber

and pushing back up the valley.
These were only the advance. In
half an hour the whole band came
jogging leisurely out of the
shadows, and little dots farther
east came streaking across the
flats to join them. Fred saw that
the whole war party was now
retracing its steps and coming
back upstream, and that now, if
he waited, he might pursue his
original intention of crossing at
the shallows, ten miles below the
mouth of the Rawhide. And so,
patiently and pluckily, he kept his
ground,—" Big Jim " contentedly
filling himself with buffalo grass
the while,—and not until the sun
was low in the west did Fred
realize their real intent. Just as
the scouts, far in advance of the

main party, reached the winding banks of the Rawhide, they seemed to hold brief consultation ; one of them plunged through to the western side, the other three turned and came straight toward the watching boy.

Great Heavens! It meant that the whole party was coming up the Rawhide, and before dark would find and follow his track. Fred's first impulse was to mount, and giving Jim the spurs, ride on the wings of the wind back to the north —back to the Niobrara, where he had left the troop in bivouac. There at least was safety, for they could not trail him in the dark. But the second thought covered him with shame. Go back—go back now ! Never, so long as he had a chance for life and hope. Away from here, and instantly, he must speed on his mission, and in another moment his girth was tightened, and " Big Jim," astonished, was racing away eastward, but keeping the sheltered ridge between him and the Platte.

CHAPTER XIII.

AWAY TO THE RESCUE!

THAT night Fred Waller slept fitfully on the open prairie, with "Big Jim" tethered close at hand. Saturday morning found him ten miles to the east and ten miles further from the river than the point where he watched the Sioux the previous evening. Hungry and worn with anxiety as he was, the poor boy's heart sank within him when he cautiously peered over the ridge into the valley. After an early

morning ride, he saw the dust
clouds near the stream, and felt
that he was still cut off. Noon
was near when, far as he could
see up or down, the valley was
clear ; and then creeping out from
his lair, he again mounted and
rode straight for the Platte.
Warily he watched in every
direction, but no intruders came.
He was spurring over the flats
only a mile from the river before
the first sign of pursuit was
made. Then, far back toward the
bluffs he had left, Fred spied a
little party of warriors coming
after him full tilt. Never stop-
ping for more than one glance he
gave Jim the rein, urging him to
full speed ; marked, as he flashed
across it only a few hundred yards

from the bank, the trail of a
cavalry command going up the
valley and wondered whose it
could be; then he and Jim went
crashing through the gravel at the
water's edge and plunged boldly
into the running stream. Deeper
and deeper brave old Jim pushed
in until the waters foamed about
his broad and muscular breast;
then Fred threw himself from the
saddle, and keeping tight hold of
the pommel and steadying his
carbine with the same hand, "Swim
for it, old man!" he shouted to
his gallant horse, and in another
minute he and Jim were floating
with the current, yet rapidly nearing the other shore. Three
minutes and, dripping wet but
safe, they were scrambling up the

south bank and speeding away
over the bounding turf with the
baffled pursuers still two miles
behind.

And these were the tracks that
Wallace found as he came hurrying back downstream.

Saturday again Fred Waller
and his faithful horse spent on the
open prairie, for in the darkness
he found it impossible to make his
way. The moon was gone by one
o'clock, and her light had been all
too faint before. But Sunday, just
a little after noon, he had come in
sight of the goal he had sought
through such infinite pluck and
peril—the Sidney road; and as
he gazed at it from afar, peering at
it as usual from behind a shelter-
ing bluff, his heart sank into his

boots.   He had come too late;
there on that distant trail were
the tiny columns of blue smoke
floating skyward which told of
burning wagons, now in crumbling
ruins.   Worse than that, here
close at hand, over on the other
side of the long, shallow swale,
were twoscore Indian warriors in
all their barbaric finery, excitedly
watching the coming of other
victims.

With a moan of anguish Fred
Waller marked, a mile beyond and
rapidly approaching them, a four-
mule ambulance with a single soldier cantering along behind.

"Oh, my God, my God!" he
groaned aloud.   "I am too late,
after all."

But the wagon halted on the

distant hills. The Indians, ab-
sorbed in their cat-like watch,
were eagerly gesticulating and
excitedly pointing to some object
far beyond. Several of their
numbers lashed their ponies into
a tearing gallop and sped away in
wide circuit to the southward,
keeping the bluffs between them
and the wagon. Others followed
part of the distance. He knew
the maneuver well; already they
were planning the surround. In
helpless agony he watched, for he
was powerless to aid—powerless
even to warn. He seized his
ready carbine, loosened the car-
tridges in his belt, and looked
eagerly to Jim's girths. Then
once again he faced the southeast,
and saw, far away across the waves

of prairie, a little puff of dust and
a little black dot—a rider—coming full tilt in the wake of the
wagon.

"Who can it be?" he wondered.
"Can he possibly know of this
ambuscade?"

All too late! A sudden flash-
ing signal from the leader, and
all at an instant with trailing
feathers, with war cry and the
thunder of a hundred hoofs, the
painted band has whirled across
the ridge in front and is down
in the dip beyond. Every Indian
has vanished from his view and
whirled into sight of the victims
on the crest beyond.

In an instant, too, Fred Waller
is in saddle, and spurring on to
the ridge which they have just

left, and then once more he reins
in where he can just peer over the
crest. He notes with a cheer of
joy that the charge is checked—
that the Indians have veered off
and are now dashing in a great
circle around the central point
on the height beyond. He sees
the wild stampede and tangle of
the mules, the overthrow of the
ambulance; the quick, cool, reso-
lute reply of the attacked. He
marks with a glow of mad delight,
of reviving hope, that there is
not a woman or child with the
party.

"Thank God!" he cries aloud,
"It isn't Mrs. Charlton." He
waves his hat with exultation as
he sees a pony stumbling in death
upon the prairie, and his rider

limping painfully away ; he knows
now that they are soldiers, holding their own for at least a time,
and that all depends on getting
aid for them before nightfall.
Far up the valley on the other
side he had marked at noon a
dust-cloud sailing slowly toward
him. It must be the Sorrels or
the Grays, hastening back to clear
the Sidney road. Here is the
thing to do : gallop back, recross
the river, meet and guide them to
the rescue. There is still time
to get them here before the sun
goes down—if only the besieged
can hold out that long.

One more glance he takes at
the stirring picture before him,
longing to drive a shot at the
nearest Indians, and as he gazes

IN FULL FLIGHT.

there comes staggering, laboring
into sight from around a point
of bluff beyond the beleaguered
party, a horse all foam and blood,
who goes plunging to earth only
a few yards away from the ambulance, and rolls stiffening and
quivering in his death agony;
but the gray-haired old rider has
leaped safely to the ground, and
his carbine flashed its instant
defiance at the yelling foe. Even
at that distance there is no
mistaking the well-known form.
Fred Waller's wondering eyes
have recognized at once — his
father.

Now indeed he speeds away
for help! Now indeed, has Jim
to run for more than life! Turning his back upon the thrilling

scene, the little trumpeter goes
like a prairie gale, whirling back
to the valley of the Platte.

.　　.　　.　　.　　.

The sun is sinking behind the
bluffs, and its last rays fall on a
bullet-riddled ambulance; on the
stiffening bodies of a half dozen
slaughtered animals—a horse and
some mules; on a grim, determined little band of soldiers—two
of them sorely wounded. The
red shafts gleam on a litter of
empty cartridge-shells and tinge
the canvas top of the overturned
wagon. Out on the rolling prairie
several hundred yards away, the
turf is dotted here and there by
Indian ponies, the innocent victims
of this savage warfare. Such
Indian braves as have fallen have

long since been picked up by their
raging comrades and borne away.
Despite their numbers, never once
yet have the savages managed to
reach the defenders. Time and
again they have swooped down in
charge only to be met by cool,
well-aimed shots that tumbled
some of their numbers to the turf
and sent the others veering and
yelling into the old familiar circle.
At last they are trying the expedi-
ent of long-range shots from different points of the compass, hoping to kill or cripple the whole
party by sundown. The bullets
clip the turf and scatter the dust
all over the ridge. There is practically no shelter, for the ground
is too hard to dig. Old Sergeant
Waller is prostrate with a bullet

through the thigh. Colonel
Gaines has bound his handkerchief tightly around his arm.
The driver lies flat on his face—
dead. Every now and then the
others turn longing eyes southward, hoping for some sign of infantry coming from the post, so
many a mile away. They know
well that Edwards will have levied
on every wagon in Sidney to
bring them; but not a whiff of
dust-cloud do they see. One of
the soldiers gives a low moan and
clasps his hands to his side; and
Cross mutters between his set
teeth, " Five minutes more of this
will settle it."

But what means this sudden
scurry and excitement among the
besiegers ? Why do they crowd

and clamor there at the north?
What can they see over that ridge
beyond the little stream? Presently others join them. Then
more and more. Then there are
whoops of rage; a few ill-aimed,
scattering shots. Three or four
of the red men ride daringly,
tauntingly down, as though to re-
sume the attack, and shout vile
epithets in vilest English in re-
sponse to the shots with which
they are greeted, and then they
too go riding away. "Lie down,
you idiots!" yells Captain Cross to
the two soldiers who would spring
up to cheer, but a moment more
and even the wounded wave their
feeble hands and join in the
triumphant shout. The ridge is
cleared of every vestige of the

foe. The warriors go speeding away eastward toward the Platte. Far out over the prairie, to the northeast, a troop of blue horsemen are driving in pursuit, and, over the neighboring crest, come a half dozen friendly forms and faces, spurring their foam-flecked horses in the race.

" Look up, sergeant ! Look up, old man ! Here's Fred himself. Didn't I tell you he was no deserter ?" It was Cross' voice, and it is Cross' strong arm that lifts the wondering, trembling veteran to his feet. The young fellow has leaped from his horse and is springing toward them. With wondrous look of relief, of inexpressible joy, of gratitude beyond all words, of almost Heaven-born rapture mingling with the sunshine in his old face, the sergeant stretches forth his trembling arms and cries aloud, "My boy! my boy!"

CHAPTER XIV.

INNOCENT OR GUILTY.

THE provost sergeant at Fort Robinson is a man who has seen and heard a great deal in the course of his army life, and who has the enviable faculty of knowing everything that is going on around him, without appearing to know anything at all. It had been his duty, a day or two previous, to expel from the limits of the reservation a rascally pack of gamblers—a species of two-legged prairie wolf

that in the rough old days on the
frontier followed every movement
of the Army paymasters, and
lured and trapped the soldiers
until every cent of their money
was gone. In point of number
the gamblers were strong enough
to take care of themselves in case
of Indian attack, yet rarely did
they venture far from the pro-
tection of the nearest troops.
Driven out of post and forbidden
to return, they had simply camped
with their whole "outfit" at the
lower edge of the military reservation, where the laws of the State
of Nebraska and not the orders
of Uncle Sam took precedence.
And here they "set up shop"
again, and had a game going in
full blast this very sunshiny Sun-

day morning, and the provost sergeant knew all about it.   He also
knew by ten o'clock that Sergeant
Dawson and Private Patsy Donovan of Charlton's troop, with some
adventurous spirits from the garrison, were down there, "bucking
their luck" against the tricks of
these skilled practitioners ; and it
was not hard to predict what the
result would be.

"Shall I take a file of the guard
and fetch them back, sir?" he
asked the colonel commanding,
and that gentleman glanced inquiringly at his cavalry friend.

"How say you, captain?"
Charlton reflected a moment and
then replied :

"No, colonel. I should say
let them have all the rope they

choose to take. I can get them when they are needed. You are sure about their whereabouts on Tuesday and Wednesday nights ?" he asked, turning to the sergeant.

"Perfectly, sir ; and just what they lost and how much they owed the quartermaster's gang when they left."

"Just see where they are at noon then, and let me know," and the provost sergeant went his way, leaving the officers in consultation.

At noon the soldier telegrapher came hurrying to the colonel and handed him a dispatch.

"I feared as much," said the old soldier as he handed the paper to Captain Charlton. "This means work for you at once. Let us go to the office; there will be dispatches from Omaha presently. Isn't it strange that no one at Sidney should have heard of the Indians getting over the Platte?"

At two o'clock Charlton's troop was in saddle, with only three familiar faces missing from the line. In the new excitement the men had ceased to speak of Trumpeter Fred. What puzzled them now was the absence of Dawson and Donovan. A sergeant sent into the garrison, to warn them that the troop was to march at once, came back to say that he had searched every stable and corral; the horses were nowhere about the post or the Agency stores, and men on guard said that they had seen the two troopers riding away

down White River soon after one
o'clock, and they had not come
back. And when Graham re-
ported them absent to Captain
Charlton, as the latter in his
familiar scouting costume rode
out to take command, the whole
troop was amazed that their leader
seemed to treat it as a matter
of no consequence whatever. He
returned the sergeant's salute and
inquired:

"Every horse fed and
watered?"

"Yes, sir."

"Every man got two days' hard
bread and bacon?"

"Yes, sir."

"How much ammunition?"

"Eighty rounds carbine per
man—twenty revolver, sir."

"Very good, sergeant;" and this brief colloquy ended, the sergeant reined about and rode to the right flank. "Prepare to mount—mount!" ordered the captain. "Form ranks!" and without further delay, "Fours right— march!" and away they went up the lonely valley, along the winding water, breaking into columns of twos and riding "at ease" the moment they had passed the point where the post commander and a little knot of officers had assembled to bid them God-speed. Captain Charlton bent down from his saddle to grasp the colonel's extended hand and whisper a few words in his ear, The colonel nodded appreciatively. "They can't escape," he answered low,

and then, watched by friendly eyes
in that little group until out of
sight, and by fierce and lurking
spies until darkness shrouded
them from view, the troop rode
jauntily on its mission; Charlton
and Blunt in murmured consultation in the lead, and forty-eight
stalwart troopers confidently and
unquestioningly following in their
tracks. Who cared that an all-
night ride through Indian-haunted
wilds was before them? It was
an old, old story to every man.

Were there "ghost lights" on
the Niobrara that night? The
Indian spies could swear by the
deeds of their ancestors that the
troop soon climbed out of the
valley of the White River and
rode briskly southward by the Sid-

ney trail, and that every man was
in his place in column when they
wound down in the "Running
Water" flats at twilight. Yet
hours afterward, far to the west,
miles away at the Laramie crossing, there were twinkling, dancing,
"firefly" gleams—like will-o'-the-
wisps—through the chinks and
loop-holes of that old log hut, and
when morning came the ground
was stamped with a fresh impress
of half a dozen set of hoof tracks—
shod horses, not Indian ponies this
time.

It must have meant "bad medi-
cine" for the Sioux, for when
morning came all the bands that
had been so confidently raiding
the trails through the settlements
found themselves compelled to

seek the shelter of their reservations. From Laramie to Sidney
the stalwart infantry came march-
ing to the scene, and from east,
north, and west the cavalry came
trotting, troop after troop, to hem
in and head them off. The very
band that ventured south of the
Platte and killed in cold blood
those helpless teamsters, and then
sought the destruction of Gaines
and his men, fleeing now before
Wallace's troops, were met and
soundly thrashed by our friends of
Company B, with Captain Charlton
and Lieutenant Blunt in the lead,
and by Monday night the broad
valley was clear of savage foes,
the cavalry were resting by their
bivouac fires, and then, from the
lips of Captain Wallace, Charlton

heard the story of Fred Waller's exploit, and of the long gallop that brought about the rescue of Colonel Gaines. Our captain could hardly wait for morning to come, but in two days more he was standing by the bedside of his old sergeant at Sidney barracks, and Trumpeter Fred was there too.

One week later, in the big, sunshiny assembly room of the old barrack, an impressive scene took place, and a long remembered though very brief trial was brought to an abrupt close. A court-martial was in session at Sidney; the general who commanded the department had himself arrived to look into the condition of affairs about the Indian reservation, and with Captain Charlton had had a

long consultation, at the close of
which the bearded, kindly-faced
brigadier had gone to the hospital
with the troop commander, and
bending over old Waller as he lay
upon the narrow cot, took his hand
and talked with him about Five
Forks and Appomattox, and then
promised him that his wish should
be respected. It was a singular
wish—a strange thing for a father
to ask. Old Sergeant Waller had
insisted that his boy should be
brought to trial before the court-
martial then in session, and con-
victed or acquitted of the double
charge of theft and desertion that
had been lodged against him. In
vain Charlton represented to him
that it was not necessary, nobody
believed the stories now; the

veteran was firm and positive in the stand he made.

"Everywhere in this department, sir, my boy's name has been held up to shame as a thief and a deserter. There is only one way to clear him; let him stand trial, prove his innocence, and let us fix the guilt where it belongs." And Waller was right.

Who that was in the court room that hot August morning, when the south wind blew the dust-cloud into the post and burned the very skin from the bronzed faces around the whitewashed wall, will ever forget the closing incidents of that trial? At the long wooden table sat the nine officers who composed the court

with their gray-haired president at
the head, all dressed in their full
uniforms, all grave and silent. At
the lower end of the table was the
keen, shrewd face of the young
judge advocate who conducted
the entire proceedings. On one
side of him, quiet, self-possessed,
and patient, sat little Fred, neat
and trim as a new pin in his fault-
less fatigue dress. A little behind
the boy was his captain, Charlton,
and along the wall, at the end of
the room, Colonel Gaines, with his
arm still in a sling, and Captain
Cross, with his piercing restless
eyes and "fighting face." On the
other side of the judge advocate
stood the chair in which witness
after witness had taken his seat
and given his testimony, and now

at high noon it was empty, and the crowd of spectators, sitting in respectful silence around the room, craned their necks and gazed at the doorway in hushed, yet eager curiosity to see the man whose name had just been passed to the orderly. It was understood that the case for the prosecution depended mainly upon his evidence.

CHAPTER XV.

IRST SERGEANT GRA-
HAM had sworn to the dis-
appearance of the money at the Niobrara and the fact that at daybreak
the trumpeter had gone with his
horse, arms, and equipments. He
also told of his belief that he and
the men who slept near him that
night had been stupefied by chloroform. Two other troopers told of
the loss of their money at the same
time ; the hospital steward from
Fort Robinson testified to Fred's

coming to him and getting a little vial of chloroform on a forged request from Sergeant Graham. Corporal Watts had positively identified a ten-dollar bill, which was in the trumpeter's possession when he was searched (at his own request) when first accused of the crime, as one stolen from him at the Niobrara. He had had some experience, he said, and had made a record of the numbers; and this record, in a little notebook, was exhibited to the court.

Not once had the defense interposed or asked a question. It was evidently the policy of Fred's advisers to let the prosecution go as far as it chose. And now came the announcement of the name that was most intimately con-

nected with the case, and Sergeant
Dawson in his complete uniform
strolled into court, removed the
gauntlet from his right hand, and
holding it aloft, looked the judge
advocate squarely in the face and
swore to tell the truth, the whole
truth, and nothing but the truth.
Then he sat down and glanced
quickly around him, but his eyes
did not seem to see Fred Waller,
nor did they rest for an instant on
Captain Charlton, who, tugging at
his mustache, looked steadily at
the face of his left guide. Then
began the slow, painful, cumbrous
method by which the law of the
land requires military courts to
extract their evidence, every question and answer being reduced to
writing. Sergeant Dawson gave,

as required, his full rank, troop, regiment, and station, but hesitated as to the latter point. "I was left behind at Red Cloud when the troop came away Sunday a week ago, sir, along with Private Donovan, and we were kept there until I got orders to come here with the hospital steward. I just got in this morning, and I'm told the troop is back at the Platte crossing." But the matter of station was of no particular consequence, and the examination proceeded. Yes, he knew the prisoner, Trumpeter Fred Waller, Troop B, and had known him several years before he had enlisted. Told to tell in his own way what he knew of the circumstances that led to the charges against Waller, the witness cleared his throat and began.

It was the night they camped at the Niobrara, giving the date, that the prisoner seemed restless. All the men expected the Indians to make an attempt to run off the horses, and all were wakeful, but he had most occasion to notice Waller, who didn't seem able to sleep. That night passed without alarm of any kind, but the next night it was very dark, the moon went down at eleven, and the horses got to stamping and snorting. Witness was sergeant of the guard, and all night long had to be moving about among his sentries and the herd. About midnight he had come in to the fire, where Sergeant Graham was

sleeping, to clean out his pipe, that
had clogged. His leather wallet,
with his money and some papers,
was inside the canvas scouting
jacket that the captain allowed
him and others of the men to
wear, and he took the jacket off a
few minutes while he walked over
to the stream and soused his head
and face in the cold water, a thing
he always tried to do when he felt
sleepy. While there he thought
he heard a call from the sentry up
the stream and he ran thither, and
it was just then that the horses
began making such a fuss. He
kept around among the sentries,
trying to find out the cause, and
did not go back to the fire until it
was all quiet after two o'clock,
and then he slipped into his jacket

and overcoat and hurried back to
where Donovan was on post below the bivouac. There was
some noise they could not understand, far out on the prairie in
that direction. He never missed
his money and the wallet until
daybreak, when it was discovered
that Waller had gone. He never
heard him steal away during the
night, and was simply amazed
when told of his desertion. The
lieutenant had been disposed to
blame him at first for letting the
trumpeter get away with his
horse, but no man could have
been more vigilant than he was.
" The captain had never blamed
him," he was sure from the captain's manner when he spoke to
him about it at Red Cloud. And

Dawson looked confidently now at his commander, but that gentleman never changed a muscle of his face.

As was customary, the judge advocate inquired if the prisoner had any questions to ask, and the spectators were amazed when he calmly answered, " No." Big beads of sweat were trickling down the sergeant's face by this time, but he could not control the look of wonderment that flashed for one instant into his eyes at this refusal of a valued privilege.

" Has the court any questions?" asked the judge advocate, and to the still greater wonderment of spectators and witness no member of the court appeared to care to inquire further. When

Sergeant Dawson left the court room and walked away toward the barracks he knew that all eyes were upon him, and just as soon as he could throw aside his saber, helmet, and full dress he lost no time in getting to the trader's store and swallowing half a tumbler of raw whisky. He thought the ordeal over and that he was free. It was with a sensation of something like premonition that, as he came forth, he saw at the barracks the orderly of the court-martial, who had been sent to warn him that he would be called by the defense at two o'clock.

CHAPTER XVI.

PRISON AND PROMOTION.

HAT afternoon the court room was crowded when Sergeant Dawson retook his seat and glanced for the first time at the prisoner before him. In front of the boy was a little table, on which was a number of slips of paper. One of these was quietly passed to the judge advocate, who took it, wheeled in his chair, and read aloud:

"What answer did you give Lieutenant Blunt when he asked

if you had been outside the sentry-line the night the prisoner disappeared ?"

" I told him that I had not, sir," was the prompt reply.

The judge advocate posted the reply on his record sheet, and wrote the answer below. Then came another slip.

" What answer did you give the captain when asked if any man had ridden back toward the Niobrara the morning the troop left there for Red Cloud ?"

The sergeant's throat seemed to clog a little, but he gulped down the obstruction. " I said no man went back, sir."

" What buildings, if any, were there near the spot where the troop was in bivouac on the Niobrara ?"

Dawson's face was losing its ruddy hue, but the beads of sweat were starting afresh.

"An old empty log hut, sir. I didn't take much notice of it, sir."

"How far from the sentries was it?"

"I don't just know, sir. Two or three hundred yards perhaps." His lips were beginning to twitch, and his eyes to wander nervously from face to face.

"How much money did you lose with your wallet that night."

"Over sixty dollars, sir.; every cent I had."

"What answer did you give Captain Charlton at Red Cloud when he asked you if you had seen anything of it since that night?"

"I told him no, sir."

"With whose money were you playing cards then, below Red Cloud, on the Sunday the troop marched away, leaving you behind?"

Dawson's face was ghastly. He choked for a moment, then seemed to make a desperate effort to pull himself together. "It wasn't so, sir," he muttered; then more loudly, "It was just a few dollars I borrowed," he began, but looking furtively around he caught one glimpse of his captain's stern face, and just beyond him, through the open window, the sight of a tall, straight form in the uniform of the infantry. It was the provost sergeant from Fort Robinson.

"It wasn't mine," he weakly murmured.

Another slip, and in the same cool, relentless tone the judge advocate read:

"What reason had you for taking your horse to the post blacksmith, instead of the cavalry farrier, to be shod the evening you reached Fort Robinson?"

Again the pallor of his face was almost ghastly, a hunted and desperate look came into his flitting eyes. One could have heard a pin drop anywhere in the court room, so intense was the silence. For the first time Dawson began to realize that his every movement had been watched, traced, and reported—and still he strove to rally.

" He was a better horse-shoer, that's all."

"You have testified that you did not go outside of the line on the night of the camp on the Niobrara, and did not allow any-one to go back after the troop marched away. For what pur-pose did you, yourself, ride back and enter the log hut you de-scribed ?"

" I—I never did," gasped Daw-son, with glaring eyes and ashen face, " I—— " but his tongue seemed to cleave to the roof of his mouth, for Captain Charlton quietly arose, stepped forward, and placed upon the table a large, flat wallet, at sight of which the sergeant's nerves gave way entirely. He made one or

two efforts to speak, he struggled
as if to rise, his eyes rolled in
his head, and in another instant
he was slipping helplessly to the
floor. A young surgeon sprang
to his side as the bystanders
strove to lift him, and with one
brief glance turned to the court:
"Mr. President, this man is in
a spasm, and should be taken to
the hospital."

"Very good, sir," was the calm
reply. "Major Edwards, will
you see to it that a sentry is
posted over him. That man
must not be allowed to escape."

Two more witnesses were ex-
amined that afternoon—the provost sergeant and Captain Charlton. The former testified that
Dawson had been gambling and

had lost heavily in the post before
pay day; that on that fateful
Sunday, bill after bill he had
seen him pay—over one hundred
dollars at the table in the gamblers' tent down below the reservation — before he interfered,
warned him of the departure of
his troop, and ordered him to
report in garrison with his horse
at once. Donovan had merely
been a looker-on at the mad game
in which the sergeant had sought
to recover his losses.

Charlton stated that, after his
investigation at Red Cloud, he
was confident that Dawson was
the trooper who rode back to
the old ranch, and that something
must be concealed there. Searching it late, Sunday night, he found

in the dugout a spot where the earth had been recently scooped away, and there in Dawson's old rubber poncho was the wallet with his papers and about two hundred dollars of the missing money, or what his men believed to be such.

And then, amid the sympathetic glances of all the court, young Fred told his strange but soldierly story. It was Dawson who asked him to get the chloroform for him at Red Cloud and gave him the folded pencil note; it was Dawson who suggested to him the idea of sleeping down below the bivouac that evening near where Donovan was posted, and it was Dawson who roused him suddenly and startlingly in the dead of the night. " Up with

you, Fred, boy!" he had said.
"Up with you, but make no noise.
There's the devil's own news!
The Indians are out everywhere!
The lieutenant's just got a courier
from Robinson, and he and Sergeant Graham have to write dispatches to go right to the captain
at Laramie. You know the
whole Platte valley, and how to
get across and reach the Sidney
road below?" Of course he did.
"Then the lieutenant says, for
God's sake lose not a minute; go
for all you're worth; keep well
to the west until you cross the
Platte, and then make for the
southeast, and warn back everybody who is coming north. He
says Mrs. Charlton and the children were to come that way,

Saturday or Sunday, to join the captain at Red Cloud. You can save them, if you're in time."

Suddenly roused from sleep, Fred was bewildered for an instant; could only realize that his loved benefactors and friends were in deadly peril and that he was chosen to haste and rescue them, Dawson lifted him into the saddle; pressed some money into his hand to buy food when he reached the settlement or Sidney, in case he met no travelers this side; led him to the water's edge, and bade him lose not an instant. He never dreamed of harm or wrong or plot until his wounded father told him the foul charge against him, after his long and gallant ride that blazing Sunday.

Then for a moment the little man broke down and sobbed; and old war-worn soldiers in the court turned away with glistening eyes, and the president, rapping on the table, huskily ordered the room to be cleared. Charlton's arms were around his trumpeter's shoulders as he led him to the open air, and to his father's bedside. "Cleared!" he said, in answer to the longing look in the sergeant's eyes. "Cleared! There isn't a man, woman, or child in all the post that doesn't know the verdict, and that Dawson is doomed to four years in prison." And then he left them together and alone.

Dawson's trial and confession settled it all. He himself was the thief, who sought in this way to

HE SOUNDED THE RETREAT.

replace the money lost in gambling and to throw upon Fred
Waller, should he escape, the
burden of the crime. But a
merciful God had watched over
the boy in his brave and loyal
effort; had guided him in safety
through a host of savage foes, and
led him on to honor and vindi-
cation in the end. For months
there was no happier boy on all
the wide frontier than the little
hero of the Sidney route; no
happier father than brave old
Sergeant Waller.

Long years afterward, riding
one evening into a cavalry camp
on the Southern plains, Captain
Cross and the writer noted a
tall, blue-eyed, bronzed-cheeked

trooper, whose twirling mustache was almost the color of the faded yellow of the chevrons on his sleeve. Despite dust and the rough prairie dress, no finer soldier had met their eyes in the long column that went flitting by.

"Who is that young first sergeant?"

"That?" answered Cross in surprise. "Don't you know who that is? Why, man, that's Charlton's old Trumpeter Fred."

THE END.

www.ingramcontent.com/pod-product-compliance
Lightning Source LLC
Chambersburg PA
CBHW030539040726
47497CB00008B/2518